THE ENCHANTED FOREST

AN EROTIC FAIRYTALE

VICTORIA RUSH

VOLUME 1

CLOVER'S FANTASY ADVENTURES -
BOOK 1

COPYRIGHT

The Enchanted Forest © 2021 Victoria Rush

Cover Design © 2021 PhotoMaras

For the uninhibited...

WANT TO AMP UP YOUR SEX LIFE?

Sign up for my newsletter to receive more free books and other steamy stuff. Discover a hundred different ways to wet your whistle!

Victoria Rush Erotica

1

Clover had always been a precocious girl. Maybe it was because she was the youngest child. Or maybe it was because she had four older brothers. Whatever the reason, she'd developed a fierce independent spirit at an early age, and it only seemed to grow stronger as she moved into her teenage years.

Now that she'd finally turned eighteen and was able to make important decisions on her own, she was beginning to rethink her future plans. Her parents had expected her to go to college once high school was over, but Clover wanted to explore the world. She'd grown tired of the rigid structure of formal education and was eager to forge her own path.

After another heated argument with her parents, she'd left the house and run out into the woods to find solitude. Growing up in the shadow of the Appalachian Mountains outside Asheville, Tennessee, she'd always loved exploring the rivers and valleys of Cherokee National Forest. There was something about the unspoiled beauty and the wild landscape that pulled her away from the city and made her want to live the nomadic life of a woodsman.

She'd always loved exploring the woods with her brothers, who'd taught her how to fish and live off the land. But now that they'd all left home to pursue greater things, she was left on her own to find amusement. Although she was beautiful with a striking figure, her brothers had protected her from the clutches of leering boys, and because she preferred to escape to the forest to seek stimulation, she hadn't made many friends.

Now, alone and unsure of the next step in her adolescent journey, she sat atop a craggy outcropping watching the sun setting over the hazy shadows of the Smoky Mountains. The purple silhouette of the undulating hills framed by the iridescent sky looked like a fantasy world a million miles away from all her troubles. But she knew her parents would begin to worry if she didn't return by nightfall, so after waiting as long as she dared, she lifted herself off the embankment and began to follow the winding creek back into town.

It was hotter than usual for this time of year, and after making her way halfway down the mountain, she stopped at a waterfall to cool off. Knowing there was nobody for miles around, she had no hesitation about removing her clothes and stepping into the cataract stark naked. She and her brothers had often skinny-dipped in the fresh rivers and lakes of Tennessee, and as she felt the pulsating water falling over her bare breasts, her hand wandered between her legs where she felt a warm tingling.

She'd always admired their athletic figures, and the older she'd become, the more she began to wonder what it would be like to feel a man's hard body pressed against her own. After discovering the pleasures of self-stimulation soon after puberty, she'd been left to her own devices to seek the pleasures of the flesh.

As she rolled her fingers over her hardening nub, she tilted her head back, approaching a powerful climax. With the rays of the setting sun twinkling in her eyes, she blinked in ecstasy from the torrent of pleasure engulfing her body. Experiencing a stronger orgasm than usual, she stumbled backwards against the rocky face of the waterfall. But instead of feeling the hard surface she expected, she collapsed onto a soft, grassy surface.

When she opened her eyes, she was surprised to see an entirely new landscape stretching for miles into the distance behind the waterfall. Instead of the familiar oak and chestnut trees of the Blue Ridge mountain range, the trees were much taller, with gleaming trunks and long, drooping branches looking like enormous willow trees. And instead of the usual ferns and loose sedge covering the ground, the new land was blanketed in bright flowers and giant toadstools, like something straight out of Alice in Wonderland.

Clover picked herself up and began strolling through the meadow with her hands out to her side, caressing the silky petals of the waist-high flowers and the soft shamrocks underfoot. The flowers had a moist feel to them, and after walking a few hundred feet, she stopped to inspect them more closely. They looked a bit like closed clams, but when she ran her fingers over their petals, they spread their wings, revealing long pistils and stamens that undulated in the late afternoon sun.

As she peered at the flowers more closely, she was struck by how much they resembled her own female anatomy. The curves and folds of the petals looked just like the lips of her vulva. They even emitted a slippery dew like her own flower, spreading further apart the more she caressed their soft outer edges and probed their inner depths. But the animated appendages fluttering *inside* the folds was definitely something she'd never seen before.

She'd learned about homosexuality in health class, and often wondered what it would be like to make love to a girl. Suddenly, she was surrounded by a field full of life-like vulvas beckoning for her to stimulate them while they spread their wings and undulated, seemingly enjoying her erotic caresses. Still moist and tingling from her orgasm under the waterfall, Clover looked around to make sure nobody was watching, then she positioned her hips over one of the plants and lowered her pussy onto the open face of the flower.

When she felt the animated fingers caressing her slit, she gasped. She'd never felt anything touching her like this before other than her own hand, and she closed her eyes imagining it was a person touching her instead of the disembodied plant. The thick and dewy pistils felt more like a tongue than a finger, and as she began to moan in rising pleasure from the erotic caress of the plant on her private parts, she lowered her hips a little further until the rigid stigma entered her hole.

As it started to stimulate the sensitive area a few inches inside, she began to flap her legs in and out, but this only seemed to cause the plant to increase the speed and pressure of the vibrating pistil. Suddenly, the long stamens surrounding the central ovule also began flapping against her sensitive bulb and lower perineum. Overwhelmed by the combination of sensations stimulating her vulva, Clover groaned feeling another orgasm wash over her, this time even stronger than the one she'd experienced under the waterfall.

When she finished climaxing, she lifted herself off the flower, watching it return to its closed clamshell appearance.

Noticing the nectar dripping around its edges, Clover swiped her finger along the crest and raised it to her mouth. The syrup tasted sweet, not unlike her own moisture when she became aroused, and she swirled it around her mouth, shaking her head in amazement at the human-like form of the flora in this strange new world.

Other than the sound of birds flitting from tree to tree in the magical forest, there was no sign of people or any other wildlife. Just the brightly colored flowers and the soft carpet of clover lining the forest floor, punctuated by the tall weeping-willow-shaped trees looking like hunched over hippies with their long hair dangling down to the ground. Even the sky seemed bluer and the sun brighter than in Tennessee, and for a moment, Clover wondered how much longer the portal would remain open.

But as she peered back at the waterfall a few hundred yards in the distance, she was in no hurry to return from this enchanted new land. As she continued wading through the field of animated flowers, she paused under one of the giant trees, feeling its soft, pendulous leaves. They felt as soft as feathers, and when she leaned in to smell them, they had a subtle minty aroma to them. She walked up to its gleaming trunk decorated with toadstools and ran her hand over the smooth, caramel-colored surface. Then she gasped when some of the toadstools began expanding and curling upward like a boy's erection.

The only time Clover had actually seen an erect cock was when she caught one of her brothers masturbating behind a tree in the woods. Just like her brother's organ, these toadstools had the same thick shaft and flaring heads. They were even roughly the same *size* as an erect penis. Curious, she reached out to touch one of the phallic-shaped objects, squeezing its spongy stem and stroking it up and down like she'd seen her brother do in the woods. As she rolled her hand over the bulbous end of the mushroom, its head became slippery with a different kind of fragrant syrup. She stooped down to flick her tongue over the flaring tip and smiled at how sweet it tasted. Unlike the salty taste of a man's semen that some of her girlfriends had talked about, this artificial penis had a pleasant taste and aroma.

As she began to bob her head up and down on the erotic fungus, imagining what it would feel like to suck a real man's cock, she felt her pussy throbbing once again. Unable to resist the growing temptation, she turned around and positioned her dripping slit over the tip of one of the toadstools and slowly lowered herself over it until it filled her cavity. Unlike the erotic flowers, which felt more like a woman's face against her cunny, this exotic plant left little doubt about its intentions. Warm, firm, and spongy, she sighed as she rocked up and down on the turgid toadstool, feeling it probing her deepest depths.

Sensing herself getting closer to the peak of her pleasure, she reached out to some overhanging branches for support, howling in delight as she felt the insides of her pussy begin pulsing in powerful contractions. After climaxing for many long seconds while holding onto the shaking branches, she couldn't help smiling at the fact that she'd finally lost her virginity to the natural wonders of the world she'd so long admired.

As she lifted herself off the toadstool, she noticed that it was coated in a new layer of fragrant dew, almost like it was trying to spread its seed. But after experiencing her third orgasm in less than an hour, Clover was too tired to begin thinking about the grand design of this strange new world. Watching the setting sun illuminating the colorful forest like some kind of fantasy fairy tale, she fell asleep with a huge smile on her face.

Her parents would have to wait a little longer for her to return to Asheville. For the first time in her life, she felt like she'd found where she truly belonged.

2

———

Clover awoke a short time later to the sound of growling surrounding her. Sitting up startled with her back against the tree, she peered into the moonlit darkness to see what was approaching her. At first, all she could see was a few pairs of yellow eyes glowering at her about ten feet away. But as her eyes adjusted to the dim light, she noticed the hulking shapes of a pack of wolves inching closer toward her.

I guess this place isn't so different from back home after all, she thought, shaking her head. *At least they appear to have some of the same animals.*

Clover paused for a moment, contemplating her options. She'd left the only weapons she could use for defense, a small hunting knife and her fishing rod, at the base of the waterfall when she removed her clothes. Now she was stark naked, her bare body glistening in the moonlight like a tempting morsel for this pack of drooling beasts. The big willow tree was too thick and smooth to climb, and by the time she reached out to the overhanging branches to move out of range, the pack would be upon her.

As she shivered looking at the closest wolf crouching down preparing to attack, she closed her eyes, frozen in fear. But just as she heard the animal leap toward her, it suddenly yelped, and she flung open her eyes, watching it run away with an arrow embedded in its haunches. Then the next nearest wolf squealed, following the first one with another arrow in its flanks. Within seconds, the rest of the pack followed its leaders into the bush, and Clover pulled her knees up to her chest, shivering in fright.

A few seconds later, she heard some rustling in the meadow a short distance away and she grabbed some branches, shaking them in front of her, trying to warn the intruder away.

"Who's there?" she said, scanning the darkness. "Don't come any closer!"

"Or you'll do what?" a pretty girl about Clover's age said, peering at her naked body saddled against the tree. "Flog me to death with those tree branches?"

Clover paused for a moment to appraise the girl. She had light blonde hair, almost white, with fair skin and large doe eyes, like a baby deer. She was shorter than Clover by almost a foot, but she had an athletic figure with full breasts and curvy hips. She wore a tight one-piece leather outfit cut off at the top of her thighs with an open vest that high-lighted her sexy cleavage. Slung over her back was a quiver full of arrows and she grasped a large home-made bow in her left hand. But her most unusual feature were two pointed ears poking out the side of her glimmering hair.

"Wh–who are you?" Clover stammered, not sure what to make of the strange woodland girl.

"I'm Tara, who are you?" she said, equally bewildered at the sight of the naked human recoiling against the base of the tree.

"I'm Clover," Clover said, still feeling shellshocked.

"You don't look like anyone from around here," Tara said, peering at the unclothed girl. "Why are you naked?"

"I was bathing in a waterfall, then something strange happened. I must have fallen through some kind of portal. I don't recognize this place at all. It doesn't look like anything from back home."

"And where's that?"

"Tennessee," Clover said, no longer hearing the sound of the waterfall in the distance. "Asheville, Tennessee. Do you know how I can find my way back there?"

"I've never heard of it. You're in the land of Abbynthia now. Do you have somewhere to go or anywhere to stay? It's not safe for you out here alone at night, especially with no protection."

"No," Clover said. "I just got here a few hours ago. I fell asleep under this tree and–"

"That's not the *only* thing you've been doing under this tree," Tara said with a sly grin.

"You've been watching me?"

"For a little while, yes. You're very beautiful, for a human."

Clover peered at the girl with a confused expression.

"You're not?"

"I'm an elf. We're a related species, but we branched off many eons ago."

"An *elf*? I thought those only existed in fairy tales."

"Well I guess you've stumbled onto one then, because I'm definitely real."

Clover shook her head to make sure she wasn't dreaming, then she stood up to brush herself off.

"Thank you for saving me," she said.

"Don't mention it," Tara said. "I couldn't let a pretty

defenseless creature like you get gobbled up by a bunch of hungry wolves. It would be a bit of a rude awakening after your exciting introduction to this new land."

"Abbynthia?" Clover said, looking at the elf with a confused expression. "Is that a part of the United States that I've never heard of?"

"The United States?" Tara said, shaking her head. "It looks like you've wandered a long way from home. I've never heard of these places you mention."

"Where can I find somewhere to shelter and get some clothes?"

"The closest town is quite some distance from here," Tara said. "But you're welcome to come back to my treehouse not too far away. It'll be safe from the wolves, and I might be able to find something for you to wear."

"That's very kind of you."

"You can wear my vest until we get there," Tara said, wrapping her cloak around Clover's shoulders. "You look like you're freezing in this night chill."

"Thank you," Clover said, realizing for the first time how exposed she appeared with her hairy muff exposed below the seam of Tara's vest.

"Come," Tara said, holding out her hand to lead Clover in the direction of the half-crescent moon. "You'd better stay close to me in case those wolves get any more ideas."

As the two girls traipsed through the meadow, Clover glanced down at the waving flowers as they opened and closed when they brushed past.

"Why were you watching me earlier?" Clover asked, following the elf's sexy round ass.

"You seemed to be enjoying yourself, and I've never seen anyone like you before."

"Am I the only one who plays with the plants this way? They're very unusual and...*erotic.*"

"No," Tara chuckled. "Many of us enjoy them in a similar manner when we're feeling needy."

"Is there a reason why they're shaped the way they are and they move like real people?"

"It's their way of propagating," Tara said. "Their form and features have evolved in such a way to make it pleasurable for those creatures with similar anatomical features to engage with them in a sexual manner. As we move from one plant to another, we carry their seeds with us to germinate the next plant."

"Like bees, you mean?"

"I don't know what bees are, but this technique has proven very effective in spreading their kind and providing useful food and nectar for the other woodland creatures."

"Not to mention spreading their *pleasure* far and wide," Clover smiled.

"Yes," Tara nodded. "They're quite stimulating, aren't they? At least when you can't find one of your *own* kind to satisfy your cravings."

"Speaking of which," Clover said, peering nervously around her in the darkness to make sure they weren't being following by the pack of wolves. "Other than you and the wolves, I haven't noticed any other sign of wildlife. Are we alone out here in the wilderness?"

"I wouldn't say *alone*, exactly," Tara said, brushing some of the overhanging branches aside as she pressed ahead. "There's plenty of less threatening creatures like rabbits and foxes out here in the forest. But in terms of humans and elves, there's no one else that I know of for many miles in either direction."

"What are you doing alone out here, like me?"

"I had a bit of a falling out with my clan," Tara said. "The chief of our village expected me to marry his son, and I didn't want any part of it. So he banished me from the group, and I started a new life for myself in the forest."

"Why didn't you want to marry his son?"

"Besides his being a pompous, overbearing ass? I dunno, I didn't feel like being anyone's property, I guess. I like being free and able to go and do as I please."

"You're stealing a page from my book," Clover laughed. "I was in a similar situation back home. My parents wanted me to go college, and I had other plans."

"College?"

"It's a type of school where older girls go to further their education. But like you, I didn't want to be tied down. I prefer exploring the forest."

"Is that what you were doing when you happened upon Abbynthia?"

"Yes. I was having a stimulating shower under a waterfall and when I slipped, I fell through some kind of portal into this strange new world."

"Do you make a habit of stimulating yourself in the forest?"

"I suppose," Clover chuckled. "But kind of like you, I've never really had a boyfriend, and this is the closest I've ever gotten to having real sex."

"We'll have to do something about that," Tara said, stopping under a large willow tree and removing an arrow from her quiver. She placed the arrow on the string of her bow and pointed it toward the base of any overhanging branch, then shot it upward. It landed with a thunk against the stem, and a knotted rope suddenly fell down from above onto the ground. Clover peered into the thick canopy of leaves and noticed a thatched hut nestled in the branches about thirty feet off the round.

"That's a pretty neat trick," Clover said, nodding at Tara's ingenuity at crafting such a hidden and safe entrance to her home.

"You can't be too careful out here," Tara said. "There's too many creatures short and tall that will take advantage of a little girl like me."

"You're not so *little*," Clover said, peering at Tara's sexy cleavage compressed by her tight leather waistcoat. "And hardly defenseless."

"Do you want to go first, or me?" Tara said, motioning to the dangling rope and pointing upward toward her treehouse.

Clover looked at the knotted vine and peered up at the base of the hut thirty feet above. She was confident in her climbing skills, but she didn't want to make a fool of herself climbing it the wrong way. Besides, she was still naked from the waist down, and she felt shy about exposing herself while the pretty elf watched her from below.

"Why don't you go first and show me the way? I'll come right after you."

"As you wish," Tara said, jumping on the vine and climbing the rope hand over hand with barely any assistance from her legs. When she got to the top, she peered down at Clover and smiled. "Well, what are you waiting for?"

Clover grabbed the vine and awkwardly shimmied up it like a climbing frog, then Tara held out her hand and pulled her inside the treehouse when she reached the top.

"Wow," Clover panted, peering around the cavernous hut. "This is quite the treefort. It's not like anything my brothers and I used to make in the woods. What did you use to build it?"

"Mostly from these medusa tree branches woven together with twine from the hanging vines. The leaves of the tree make a waterproof thatch overhead and also serve to disguise the presence of my house up here off the ground."

"That's amazing that you're able to build such as sturdy structure without any hammers and nails," Clover said, shaking her head. "You're a real woodsman, or whatever's the proper name for a female elf who knows how to look after herself alone in the forest."

"Are you hungry?" Tara said, opening a cupboard full of strangely colored fruits and vegetables. "How long has it been since you've eaten?"

"I hadn't realized how hungry I was until you mentioned it. It's been at least twelve hours since I've had anything."

"Here," she said, passing Clover a small citrus fruit and a gourd that looked a bit like an eggplant. "This should give you some quick energy and fill your belly for a little while."

Clover dug her fingernails into the skin of the fruit and peeled off the husk, peering at the strange blue color of the flesh.

"What kind of plant is this?" she said, pinching her eyebrows. "We don't have anything like this back home."

"It's a chukruss," Tara said. "Very sweet and very nutritious. Give it a try, it won't bite you."

Clover sunk her teeth slowly into the side of the fruit, then her eyes widened as she hummed in satisfaction.

"It's very tasty," she nodded. "This place is full of surprises."

Then she picked up the oblong eggplant-looking vegetable and turned it around in her hand.

"What about this one? Is this another one of those dual-purpose plants that you use for sexual gratification?"

"Well, I suppose you could use it that way in a pinch," Tara smiled. "But we normally prefer to *eat* it. We call it inkberry. You can eat it with the skin and all. It has lots of good fiber."

Clover chomped down over the narrow end of the vegetable, nodding approvingly.

"Tastes a bit like a squash," she nodded. "A very tasty and succulent squash."

When she'd finished two more of the chukruss fruit and another purple tuber, she peered over at Tara with her face and hands dripping from the juices of the succulent fruit.

"Do you have a napkin or something for me to clean up with?"

Tara pulled a cloth from a nearby cupboard then dipped it in a bowl of water resting on the sink. Then she leaned over toward Clover, raising the cloth to her face.

"Here," she said, bringing her face closer to Clover's. "Let me help you with that."

As she began gently wiping Clover's face, the two girls peered into each other's eyes and hesitated. Then they pressed their lips together and intertwined their tongues as they fell onto the thatched floor, pulling off their clothes. For the next hour or so, the two sexually starved girls pressed their bodies together, licking and sampling their unusual shapes and forms, writhing and moaning in pleasure before falling asleep in each other's arms.

3

———

A warm breeze wafting through the open window of Tara's treehouse woke Clover, and she peered over at the elf preparing some food in her makeshift kitchen. She was completely naked, and for the first time, Clover had a chance to view her body in the daylight. Although she was shorter than Clover, her body was in similar proportion to hers, with a firm tight ass, a narrow waist, and a taut, athletic figure. Clover felt a stirring in her loins recalling how the two of them had fallen into each other's arms the previous night, and as she sat up on the thatched mat, Tara turned around and smiled at her.

"Good morning! Did you sleep well?"

"Better than last time, that's for sure. I'd far prefer waking up *this* way than surrounded by wolves."

"Although you were doing your *own* fair share of growling last night," Tara said, handing her a wooden plate with some peeled fruit and dried meat. "You must be hungry after all that exercise."

Clover smiled at Tara as she tore a chunk off the meat, running her eyes over the elf's bare tits and pointed nipples.

"You're even more beautiful and sexy in the daylight," she said, gulping down the jerky. "What kind of meat is this? It's tastes different than the dried meat I'm used to."

"Lamb. Do you like it?"

"Yes," Tara said, beginning to realize that this mythical land of Abbynthia wasn't so different from back home after all. "But where do you get it? I didn't see any sheep or lamb on our way to your cabin last night."

"I pick up a few provisions in the market every fortnight or so. It's a bit of a hike to the nearest town, so I mostly make do with naturally grown fruits and vegetables in the meantime."

"How do you *pay* for things around here? Do you have some kind of job?"

"I'm a trapper. I hunt and trade animals like beaver, grouse, and rabbit for larger domestic animals and the occasional eggs and milk."

"You seem to be pretty self-sufficient out here all by yourself in the woods," Clover said, peering around the airy treehouse. "Do you ever get lonely?"

"I hadn't really thought much about it until I met you. You've been a welcome–um–*distraction* beyond my usual foraging and hunting."

Clover picked up a curved inkberry vegetable and caressed it teasingly between Tara's legs.

"Are you saying you prefer making love to *humans* over these exotic plants?"

"Possibly," Tara smiled, leaning in to kiss her new friend. "You make love pretty well for someone who's never done it before. I mean, for a *human*..."

Clover placed her food tray beside her and scrunched up closer to the Tara, wrapping her legs around her hips as she pressed her bare breasts against the elf's.

"You're pretty good, yourself," she purred, feeling Tara's nipples hardening as they slapped their tits together. "For a *girl*."

"Oh yeah?" Tara grinned, rubbing her moistening crotch against Clover's soft bush. "You like rubbing your pussy against my cunny?"

"It's warmer than those *flowers*, that's for sure," she grunted, pulling Tara closer as they wrapped their legs around one another and began kissing passionately.

As the two girls began to rock their hips together, they groaned into each other's mouths, savoring the feel of their smooth bodies and slippery flesh. Clover arched her back and tilted her head back, groaning in pleasure, and Tara took the opportunity to nibble on her neck and suck one of her erect nipples into her mouth.

"Uhnnn," Clover grunted. "I love the way you make love to me."

"Enough to stick around a little longer?" Tara grinned. "Or are you still eager to go back home?"

"Not right *now*, that's for sure."

As the two girls began to rock their hips together, the sound of their intermingling juices filled the cabin, and they peered into each other's eyes as their mouths began to gape open on the crest of climax.

"Nnghh," Tara groaned, jerking her body in spastic convulsions as Clover felt her own orgasm wash over her.

While the two women clasped onto each other, the only sound in the isolated cabin was the crunching of the thatched mat beneath them and the sloshing of their flapping pussies against one another. When they both finished climaxing, they fell onto the mat together as Tara traced her fingers down Clover's heaving torso.

"Do *all* humans have this color hair?" she said, twirling her fingers in Clover's moist auburn-colored pubic hair.

"No," Clover said. "Some have fair hair like yours, some have brown or black hair, and a few have reddish colored hair like me."

"So you're *special*, then?"

"I suppose so," Clover said. "Do you like it?"

"It suits you," Tara nodded. "It makes you look exotic and sexy. Especially when my face is buried in your bush."

"Mmm," Clover said, rolling over to plant a wet kiss on Tara's lips. "I'll never get tired of that."

"There'll be time for more of this later," Tara said, suddenly sitting up. "Right now, we should collect some more food and look into getting you dressed. You can't run around buck naked like that all day."

"Why not?" Clover teased. "Who *else* is looking besides a few hungry wolves?"

"You never know who we might run into in these woods. You don't want to look too tempting a target for any passing scoundrels."

"But I've got *you* to protect me, right?" Clover said, rubbing her face against Tara's neck playfully.

"Yes, but you're going to need to learn how to protect yourself if you're going to hang around here very long. Do you know how to use a bow and arrow?"

"I've tried using my brothers' crossbow a couple of times, but nothing like yours."

"I don't know what that is, but we'll practice using my bow a little later. Right now, let's find you something to wear. As delicious as you look naked, you'll get eaten alive by the mosquitos if you go traipsing through the woods like that."

"Great, *mosquitos*," Clover sighed. "Just when I was beginning to think I'd found paradise."

Tara got up and opened a cupboard on the far wall and pulled out a half-tunic shaped like the one Clover saw her wearing yesterday.

"You're a little taller than me, but otherwise we seem to have fairly similar proportions. This is made out of sheepskin, so it will stretch to fit you over time. Why don't you try it on?"

Clover got up and took the garment from Tara's hand and turned it around, trying to figure out how to get into it. Unlike the cargo shorts and flannel shirts she was used to wearing in Tennessee, this wasn't like anything she'd seen before.

"You put your legs through these holes," Tara said, holding the open face of the vest away from Clover.

She stepped into the bodysuit, and Tara pulled it up tight over her hips and ass, then she held one of Clover's hands and threaded it through one of the arm holes. It fit snugly on Clover's taller body, but the natural fabric caressed her body like soft suede, and she smiled as she began to move her arms around, feeling the fabric stretch with her. Tara smiled approvingly, then she began to lace up the front of the bodice until Clover's breasts were tightly compressed under the center seam.

"Do I have to be tied into this thing so tightly?" she said.

"We don't want your tits flopping out at an inopportune time," Tara said. "Like when we're running away from wolves or having a drink in the local tavern. You're already plenty alluring enough with that flaming red hair and pretty freckles without needing your more fulsome features attracting additional attention."

"I'm not quite sure this skimpy outfit is going to exactly scare any leering men away," Clover said, peering down at her compressed breasts spilling over the top of her leather corset.

"It'll have to do for now," Tara said. "We can try to make you something more comfortable later. "For now, let's see if we can replenish our supplies and start making you into a real woodsman, or whatever you call human girls that explore the forest."

The two girls lowered themselves from the cabin on the knotted vine, then Tara pulled one of the low overhanging branches, swinging the rope back to the top of the canopy.

"You've just got the *one* room to live in?" Clover said, peering up to see how well Tara had camouflaged her tree-house from the view on the ground. "I mean, where do you go pee and do your other business?"

"Where all the *other* forest creatures go–in the forest."

"Do you use toilet paper?"

"Toilet what?"

"You know, to wipe your bum after you're finished."

"I rub myself against a mossy tree or wash myself in a local stream whenever I feel the need. But I think you'll find this forest diet keeps you pretty clean. You don't see any bears and wolves wiping their ass, do you?"

"You've got *bears* here too?"

"And lions and dragons, depending on how far you travel in Abbynthia."

"*Dragons*?" Clover said, widening her eyes. "That's so cool, I've never seen one of those before."

"Like they only exist in fairy tales?"

"Something like that."

"Shh!" Tara whispered, suddenly motioning for Clover to crouch down beside her as she pointed to a furry animal scurrying through the brush. "I'm going to show you how to spear a rabbit. Watch closely, then you can give it a try."

Tara kneeled quietly in the grass, then she raised her hand over her shoulder to her quiver, slowly pulling out a single arrow. She placed it on the string of the bow, then she pulled the string back, tensing her arm as she angled her bow in the direction of the darting rabbit. When it paused to munch on a leafy plant, Tara released the arrow and it flew through the air, spearing the animal through its shoulders. The rabbit squealed and flopped over onto its side, squirming in pain. Tara rushed up to the wounded animal, then pulled a hunting knife out of her side holster, slicing its head off in one quick motion.

Clover gasped as she pulled up beside Tara, staring at the limp and bleeding carcass.

"*What*?" Tara said, looking at Clover surprised. "You've never killed a rabbit before? What kind of forest-dwelling creature are you?"

"I usually let my brothers do the hunting when I go exploring. I only know how to fish..."

"Well at least you're good for *two* things so far," Tara grinned. "But you should learn how to use a bow and arrow too. You never know when you might need it to defend yourself, like with the wolves last night."

She paused as she pointed toward a mossy tree about fifty feet away.

"Look, there's another one," she said, handing Clover her bow and taking another arrow out of her quiver. "Now you try it."

Clover looked in the direction she was pointing and noticed another rabbit foraging in the brush. She placed the arrow on the bow like she'd seen Tara doing earlier, then she pulled it back, closing her eyes.

"You're going to need to open your eyes if you want to hit the target," Tara whispered into her ear.

"But it's so *cute!*" Clover said.

"You eat meat, don't you?"

"Yes..."

"Well then, you're going to need to learn how to *kill* it too. I can't do everything for you."

Clover opened her eyes and took aim at the rabbit, shaking her bow nervously in her hand. Then she released the string and the bow flapped against her arm with the arrow falling down onto the ground between her legs.

Tara peered at her like she was a helpless baby, then she picked up the arrow and handed it back to her.

"You're *thinking* about it too much," she said. "Don't release the tension so slowly. Instead of *lifting* your fingers off the string, slide them over. That releases the tension more quickly and makes the arrow fly true. Try it again."

Clover placed the arrow back in the bow, then pointed it around the clearing until she found another rabbit. This time, she slipped her fingers off the tensed string, and the arrow shot out in the direction of the animal. But it landed a few feet to the side, and the rabbit scurried under a fallen log.

"Better," Tara said, nodding. "It takes a bit of practice to find your aim. Try it again."

It took another five tries until Clover managed to catch the leg of one of the rabbits, then Tara showed her how to slice its neck to quickly put it out of its misery. They collected three more rabbits before the sun rose high overhead, then they stopped to build a fire, where Tara showed Clover how to skin and dress the animals to roast them over a makeshift spit.

"Not bad for your first day," Tara nodded, watching Clover tear into the freshly baked meat as they sat cross-legged facing one another. "Does it taste better after you've caught it yourself?"

"It tastes pretty damn good," Clover said, licking her lips.

"Good enough to get over your hesitation to kill it?"

"It might take me a while to develop your cutthroat attitude, but I'll get there eventually."

"So you're thinking of sticking around Abbynthia a little longer? Or are you planning to return to Tennessee United States?"

"I hadn't really thought about it, to be honest," Clover said. "I've been so distracted ever since I got here. But it would be good to know how I can get back when I need to. My parents will be worrying about me. Can you take me back to the meadow where you found me to see if the portal is still there?"

"Sure," Tara said, smiling at her new friend. "But are you sure you want to go back there just to find the *waterfall*?"

"Are you referring to the erotic flowers?" Clover said. "Why do I need those when I have *you*?"

"You never know when we might get separated. Besides, who said I was going to *keep* you? I've been managing just fine all alone all this time."

"*What*?" Clover said, looking at Tara with a hurtful expression. "You don't want me anymore? What about this morning and last night?"

"Don't get your knickers in a knot," Tara said, reaching out to squeeze Clover's hand. "You're beginning to grow on me. And now that you've learned how to hunt, you're useful to me in *other* ways."

4

———

After their lunch of roast rabbit and wildberries, Tara and Clover headed back in the direction of the waterfall. Clover's plan was to go back to Asheville just long enough to tell her parents that she was okay and that she planned to go on a long hitchhiking trip. If she told them she'd found a hidden portal to a fantasy world, they'd lock her up in a mental institution. But when they reached the waterfall, Clover was alarmed to find that on the other side there was only an impenetrable wall, no gateway back to Tennessee.

"*Now* what?" she said to Tara. "I can't stay here forever. My parents will have the entire National Guard out searching for me if I don't return soon."

"Are you sure this is the same waterfall?" Tara said.

"Unless you know of another one nearby. I didn't stray far before I fell asleep next to the tree."

"This is the only one that I know of in the area. Did you do anything differently when you came through from the other side?"

"I was just having a refreshing shower, then I stumbled

backwards through the portal."

"Are you sure you were only having a *shower*?" Tara said, arching an eyebrow.

"Well, now that you mention it, I was touching myself while I was under the water. And it was only after I climaxed that I fell through the portal."

"Maybe that's the secret," Tara smiled. "Maybe you have to stimulate yourself to orgasm to unlock the magic powers of the portal."

Clover peered at Tara with a wrinkled forehead.

"Do you really think so?"

"It's the only thing you did differently. If you're sure this is the same waterfall."

"I suppose it's worth a try," Clover said, shaking her head.

As she removed her tunic and turned back toward the waterfall, Tara reached out and grabbed her hand.

"What if you can't come back?" she said. "I've grown quite fond of you in the short time we've been together. I'd hate to find that you've gone forever and that we'll never see each other again."

"If it works both ways, then I shouldn't have any trouble getting back. I won't be gone for long, maybe just a day or two." She pulled Tara close to her, giving her a warm embrace. "Don't worry, I feel the same way about you. This place has grown on me too."

Clover ducked back under the cascade and placed her hand between her legs, rolling her button between her fingers, but she had a hard time getting aroused. Whether it was because of the pressure she felt having to climax or because she wasn't in the mood, she wasn't sure. But something definitely was holding her back from experiencing the same pleasure she'd felt the last time she was under the waterfall. After five minutes or so of rubbing herself to no avail, she stepped out of the waterfall, shaking her head at Tara.

"What happened?" her friend said. "It didn't work?"

"I couldn't come. I just didn't feel the same kind of excitement that I did the first time."

"Maybe you don't really *want* to go back," Tara said. "Your mind can play tricks on you when you're thinking of other things."

"Maybe," Clover said. "Or maybe I just need a little help. Will you come under the water with me? I'm pretty sure I won't have any trouble getting in the mood with you providing a little extra stimulation."

"What if I get pulled back *with* you?" Tara said. "I'd hate to get stuck in your world. I'm not sure they'd look kindly on a strange elf like me."

"If the trick to passing through is climaxing under the water, all you have to do is be careful not to stimulate yourself too much. Just focus on helping *me*."

"I think I can manage that," Tara smiled.

Clover reached out to take Tara's hand, pulling her toward the falling water.

"Okay, just do what you normally do. It shouldn't take long this time."

As the two girls lowered themselves under the cataract, they pressed their bodies together and kissed each other passionately. While Clover pressed her hand between her legs and began to play with her hardening bean, Tara squeezed her buttocks, grinding her mound against the back of Clover's flapping hand. This time, it didn't take Clover long to feel the pleasure building up within her, and when she climaxed, she let herself fall back toward the other side of the waterfall. But once again, she felt nothing but hard rock.

When the two girls pulled themselves out of the cascade, Tara peered at Clover with a wrinkled brow.

"Well? Did you *come* this time? What did you feel on the other side?"

"Oh, I came alright," Clover said. "But it was the same result. Just a hard stone wall, no portal."

"Hmm," Tara said. "We seem to be stuck between a rock and a hard place."

"Don't make jokes about this," Clover said, punching Tara's shoulder playfully. "I'm really worried now. What if I can never get back?"

Tara paused for a moment to consider their options. Then she peered up at Clover with a glimmer in her eye.

"There had to be some kind of *magic* involved to get you here in the first place, right?"

"I suppose so. A portal to another world isn't exactly a natural phenomenon..."

"Well, if it takes magic to make it work, maybe we need the help of a magician to figure it out. I've heard of a warlock a couple of villages over. Maybe he can help us."

"Okay," Clover nodded. "I suppose it couldn't hurt. We don't have much more to go on at this point. Can we go there right away?"

Tara peered at Clover still shivering with her wet hair and wrapped her vest around her to keep her warm.

"Why don't we rest up for a few minutes while we dry off and have something to eat? It's a bit of a long journey."

"Do we have any more rabbit left over from this morning?" Clover said, suddenly feeling her stomach grumbling.

"I'm afraid not," Tara said, peering around the clearing. "But we shouldn't have too much trouble finding some food here. The mushrooms are edible, and there's some chukruss fruit growing near the top of the medusa tree."

As the girls began walking through the meadow of erotic plants, Clover couldn't help caressing the tops of the vulva-shaped flowers and phallic-shaped mushrooms. Remembering how much fun she'd had playing with them on her first day, she began to feel another stirring in her loins.

"This one's got enough for *both* of us," Tara said, stopping at a two-headed toadstool standing at hip height.

"*Mmm*," Clover said, caressing the dewy tips of the forked fungus. "Are you sure you want to *eat* it? Maybe we can enjoy it another way first."

"You're a dirty girl, aren't you?" Tara said, peering at Clover's still dripping breasts spilling over the top of her tight bodysuit.

"I'm still feeling aroused from that stimulating shower under the waterfall. Don't you feel like having a little fun, too? You must have gotten a little worked up under the waterfall. And unlike me, you didn't have a chance to release your sexual tension."

"Now, that you mention it, I *am* feeling a little itchy," Tara said, peering at Clover with a lopsided grin.

Clover pulled the two tips of the tall toadstool apart then watched them spring back together like two frotting penises.

"And this is one of those erotic plans we can enjoy *together*," she said. "Come on, let's give it a try!"

"You're twisting my arm," Tara said, pulling off her clothes.

The two girls stood naked facing one another over the two-headed mushroom, then they smiled at one another while their hands drifted between their legs to angle the tips into their holes. As they lowered their bodies onto the sturdy stalk, they both groaned feeling the spongy projections filling their depths.

"Unngh," they grunted, leaning towards one another, intertwining their tongues.

The tall toadstool was surprisingly sturdy, and as they bobbed their hips up and down on it, it swayed and flexed along with their body weight. With their tits and mounds pressed up against one another while they fucked the tumescent fungus, they moaned into each other's mouths feeling their pleasure rising together in lockstep.

"God damn, I love this magical land," Clover smiled.

"Who needs a portal when you've got *these* things to keep you amused all day long?" Tara nodded, digging her fingernails into Clover's back as she felt her pleasure nearing the tipping point.

"*Come* with me, Tara," Clover panted. "I'm getting close. Let's fuck this thing like there's no tomorrow."

"For all we know, there might not be one, " Tara grunted, feeling her floodgates opening. "Fuck, I'm *coming*! This is so much better with two people!"

"Nnngh," Clover groaned, feeling her body beginning to convulse over the twitching fungus.

As the two girls clamped onto one another threshing and wailing atop the waving toadstool, they rolled their tongues in each other's mouths, panting in simultaneous ecstasy. When they finally finished cumming together and lifted themselves off the dripping plant, Tara wrapped her hand around Clover's side of the mushroom, ripping off the tip and crunching on the fleshy fungus, licking her lips at the taste of her girlfriend's nectar. Clover did the same, and as they stood grinning at one another like two teenagers in a brothel, she shook her head.

Now they're never going to believe me when I tell them what I found in this place, she thought.

5

After Clover and Tara had their fun on the two-pronged toadstool, they ate some chukruss and wildberries to replenish their energy before setting out for the warlock's village. It was almost a full day's hike, and by the time they entered the hamlet of Crowhollow, it was nearing dusk. As they strolled up the main strip, Clover peered around at the odd collection of old wooden buildings.

Like an old frontier town, weathered shop signs carried names like Blacksmith, Apothecary, and Dry Goods. Horses pulling rickety old carriages trundled up the dusty street, and townspeople wearing tanned hides peered out at the curious newcomers from wooden chairs on their front porches.

"This looks like something straight out of the *Wild West*," Clover said, sidestepping some piles of horse manure scattered along the main thoroughfare. "I guess it's too much to wish for an ice cream parlor or a hamburger stand?"

"The closest ice is at the top of Mount Haverhorn, hundreds of miles to the north. And I don't know what a hamburger is, but we should be able to get some hot grub at the saloon just up a ways."

Tara paused as she watched two drunken men stumbling out the front door of the tavern.

"Keep your wits about you when we go in this place," she said, bracing her arm in front of Clover's chest. "It'll be full of gamblers, drifters, and other shady characters this time of day. Let me do most of the talking."

"Okay," Clover said, suddenly realizing how vulnerable she felt without any weapon.

The two women entered the front door of the noisy saloon, and within seconds the din dropped to a whisper as the patrons peered at the scantily clad girls. Tara found an empty table near the back of the room, and motioned for the bar maid to bring them some drinks. A curvy girl wearing a short dress ambled up to their table and smiled at the newcomers.

"What can I get you girls?" she said, staring at Tara's pointy ears.

"Two ales and a pork-belly sandwich", Tara said, dipping into her side pouch and placing a copper coin on the table.

The waitress picked up the coin and flipped it over, then nodded as she headed back into the kitchen. While she was gone, Tara looked around the room, noticing everybody staring at them.

"Is it just *me*," Clover said. "Or do we stick out like purple unicorns in this place?"

"We might as well be," Tara nodded, unflapping her knife holster. "They probably don't get many elfs in here, and you look like you're from a whole other place altogether."

"Which I kind of am," Clover sighed. "Is it safe for us in here with all these leering customers?"

Tara glanced up at the balcony where a stream of men paraded up and down the hallway with young women on their arms.

"Fortunately, this saloon also has a brothel on the upper floor. So at least they have another distraction to satisfy their prurient interests if need be."

"I've never been in a brothel before," Clover said, smiling at some of the girls as they led the men into their private quarters.

"And we don't want to *stay* in one for very long," Tara said, noticing some of the men leering at Clover's exposed legs. "You're too tempting a target for these randy scoundrels. I'm sure the madam or whoever runs this operation would love to get her claws into you. You'd probably double their profits overnight."

"What about *you*?" Clover said. "You're just as pretty as me. Surely you look just as out of place and tantalizing as me."

"I'm carrying a quiver of arrows and a large hunting knife," Tara said, staring down some of the leering men. "They wouldn't want to mess with me. They can tell I know how to look after myself."

"Speaking of which," Clover said. "Shouldn't I be carrying a weapon too? Apparently it's not just the *wolves* that I need to be worried about."

"We can look into getting you something before we leave town," Tara nodded. "It would be good for both of us to have protection."

The waitress returned to their table with a tray of beers and their sandwich, placing them on the table.

"Can I get you girls anything else?"

Tara leaned in closer to the barmaid and lowered her voice.

"There was one other thing," she said. "I heard there was a warlock in these parts. I don't suppose you know where I can find him?"

The waitress peered at Tara for a long moment while she glanced around the room nervously.

Tara reached into her pouch, sliding two more copper coins across the table.

"You must be talking about Aramiss," the waitress said, picking up the coins. "I heard he lives in a cabin a couple of miles north of town. Look for an orange brick house with a green roof."

"Thank you," Tara said as the barmaid scurried to another table.

"That wasn't too hard," Clover said, picking up one of the glasses of ale and coating her upper lip with its frothy foam.

"That was the *easy* part," Tara said, taking a swig of her beer and passing the sandwich plate in Clover's direction. "The hard part will be getting the warlock to divine the location of your mysterious waterfall."

"You're not hungry?" Clover said, picking up the sandwich and taking a big bite. "This is actually pretty good."

"I just want to get the hell out of this place as soon as we can. We're sitting here like sitting ducks."

Before Clover could finish her sandwich, two drunken ratcatchers wandered over to their table, plopping themselves down in the two empty chairs.

"What do we have here, Elias?" one of the men said, leering at Tara's plump cleavage. "A pretty little pixie and some fresh ginger?"

"Aye, Ollie," the other man said, licking his lips. "I'd like to sink my pole into her tight little quim. Though I'm not sure it would fit all the way in, as tiny as she is and all."

"No doubt," the first man said. "Although this tall one looks plenty robust enough to satisfy both of us."

"We don't want any trouble," Tara said, drifting her hand down to her side.

"*Trouble*?" the first man said. "We're not looking for trouble, are we Elias? We're just looking for a bit of fun. How long's it been since you girls had a real man stuff your gusset?"

"Not long enough," Tara said, wincing at their foul stench. "Not that either of you reprobates look man enough to satisfy any woman."

"Now look here, you little tramp," the first man growled, sliding his hand across the table toward Tara.

Suddenly she pulled her knife out from her side and slammed it down hard on the wooden table between the man's fingers. He paused, looking up at her surprised, then the other man lurched across the table toward her. Tara pulled an arrow out of her quiver with her other hand and thrust the pointy end against the man's neck, pressing it hard against his windpipe.

"Do you perverts *still* think you've got the wherewithal to give us anything we need?" she sneered as the second man gagged on the arrowhead.

The ringleader hesitated for a moment, peering over at Clover, who was doing her best trying to look as threatening and resolute as Tara.

"Come on, Elias," he said, withdrawing his hand. "These bitches wouldn't be any fun in the sack anyhow. They're probably queer. Wearing those outfits, they wouldn't know what to do with a man's cock."

"Suits me just fine," the sidekick said, trembling in fear as she continued holding the sharp tip of her arrow against his carotid artery.

Tara pulled the spear back then quickly placed it in her bow, pointing it toward the two men.

"You better watch your step around these parts," the first man said, backing away from the table. "It's not safe for two girls alone in this town. There's a lot more where we come from."

"I hope you come better prepared next time," Tara rasped. "I've stopped far worse than your kind in my day. The woods are full of fearsome creatures like me. You're not the only one who should mind his manners around here."

Tara stepped away from the table, motioning for Clover to follow.

"Come on, Clover," she said. "Let's blow this pop stand. We've got more important business to attend to."

Clover pulled the heavy hunting knife out of the table and waved it in front of her as the two girls tiptoed past the tables of surprised onlookers until they exited out the front door.

"*Damn*, Tara," Clover said, when they stepped outside. "That was *bad ass*! Apparently it's not just wolves you know how to scare off!"

"We got a bit lucky in there," she said, shaking her head. "Those low-lifes were too drunk to be any serious danger. But if they had any more pals with them, we mightn't have gotten out of there so easily. I think you're right about getting you better equipped. Do you have a preference for a weapon?"

"How about a *shotgun*?" Clover said, still trembling from the frightening experience.

"What's that?"

"You don't have *guns* here in Abbynthia? It's a metal barrel that fires pellets that can kill a man from hundreds of feet away."

"That sounds like a pretty handy device," Tara nodded. "But we don't have anything like that in Abbynthia. We could go to the blacksmith to see if he can make you a new knife or a sword. Although judging by the way you were wielding my knife in there, I'm not sure that's the best choice."

"What about a bow and arrow like yours? I'd rather keep my adversaries at arms' length, so I don't have to smell their foul odor."

"You still need a bit of practice to become competent using a bow," Tara said. "Besides, it would be better for you to carry a different weapon so we've got more flexibility handling special circumstances. Come with me, I have an idea."

The girls walked a short distance down the main drag, then Tara led Clover into a store marked Tannery.

"Hello," Tara said, walking up to the counter where an old man stood, buffing some hides.

"Hello," he said, peering at the two girls curiously. "What can I do for you ladies?"

"Do you carry bullwhips?" Tara said.

"I think I have one or two in the back," the man said. "I haven't been asked for one of those in a long while. Whatever do two pretty girls like you want with one of those? You don't exactly look like the rancher type."

"Protection," Tara said.

The old man nodded, then excused himself as he went into the rear of his store. When he returned, he carried a thick, snake-like leather strap bundled in a coil.

"Is *this* the sort of thing you're looking for?" he asked, handing it to Tara.

Tara took the strap from his hand and uncoiled it,

feeling its weight in her hand as she waved it up and down slowly.

"Here," she said, handing it to Clover. "You try it."

"What exactly am I supposed to do with it?" she said, flapping it from side to side.

"You aim it at something, then snap your hand to make it straighten out and crack at the tip." Tara pointed to a wooden sign hanging on the far wall. "Try hitting that. I shouldn't create too much damage."

Clover peered at the target about twenty feet away then she flapped her arm like she'd seen Indiana Jones do in the movies, and the whip see-sawed sideways, tipping a bottle off the wall over the proprietor's head. He ducked just in time to catch the falling object, looking at the two women like they were fresh off the boat.

"Sorry about that," Tara said, passing the man a handful of coins. "Will this take care of the cost?"

"That should do it," he nodded. "But you girls be careful with that thing. You could take someone's eye out with that thing if you're not careful."

"That's the idea," Tara said, coiling Clover's whip back up and attaching it to her belt as she headed back out the door.

"Sorry," Clover said when they exited the store. "It looks like I'm a bit of a slow learner when it comes to using all these medieval tools."

"Don't worry," Tara said, noticing the two ratcatchers staring at them from the tavern porch. "We'll get you trained up soon enough. Right now, I think its best we clear out of this place and head toward the warlock's house. It's getting dark, and there'll be new matters to deal with before long."

6

The two girls continued up the dusty road heading north as the bar maid had indicated, but by now it was pitch black outside and it was difficult to make out the color of any buildings. Many of the houses were set back some distance from the road, and as they squinted into the inky darkness, Clover shook her head in frustration.

"How are we ever going to find the warlock's house in *this* light?" she said. "Haven't you guys ever heard of electricity?"

"What's that?"

"It's a kind of man-made power that creates artificial light and..." Clover paused, realizing how insane she must have sounded trying to explain all the modern conveniences she'd taken for granted to people stuck in an older time. "Never mind."

"He's a *warlock*, right?" Tara said. "So he probably has a lot of people coming to him for help. And I'm guessing he doesn't do it for free. He probably lives in a bigger house than most people around here. You keep your eyes on houses on the left side of the road, and I'll scan the right side."

After another mile or so, Clover noticed the outline of a large two-story building set back a hundred feet or so from the main road, surrounded by a tall copse of trees.

"This place looks a little larger than most of the others," she said, pausing at the side of the road and pointing into the thicket.

"Yes," Tara nodded. "And it's about the right distance from town. Let's check it out."

The girls tiptoed up the stony pathway, not wanting to alarm the inhabitant of the house with the appearance of late-night intruders, then paused outside the front door. Tara swiped her hand across the rough brick exterior, then rubbed her fingers together in the moonlight.

"It looks rusty-colored to me," she said. "This is as good a possibility as any."

She stepped forward and rapped the steel door knocker, and they heard some heavy footsteps approaching from inside. Someone pulled the curtains aside, then the door opened slowly.

"Are you the warlock, Aramiss?" Tara said, peering up at a tall bearded man wearing heavy robes.

"Maybe," he said. "Who wants to know?"

"My friend and I need some assistance, and we were hoping you could help. May we come in?"

The man peered at the young girls in their revealing costumes, then he opened the door a little further, motioning for them to come inside. In one corner of the lower level sat a small kitchen with a wooden table, but most of the room was filled with floor-to-ceiling bookcases lined with leather tomes and bottles filled with mysterious ingredients. The man motioned for the girls to take a seat in two upholstered chairs around the fireplace, then he went to the kitchen to fetch some tea. When he returned, he placed the cups on the table in front of them and sat down on a large rocking chair next to the fire.

"What can I do for you ladies?" he said, tilting his teacup up to his lips.

"So you're Aramiss, the warlock?" Tara said, making sure they'd found the right place.

"In the flesh," the man nodded, peering at them over the rim of his cup.

"My friend seems to have lost her way," Tara said. "We think she fell through some kind of portal while hiking in the woods. She comes from a different world."

"Does your friend have a name?"

"Sorry, my name's Tara and this is Clover."

"How did you two find each other?" the warlock said, glancing at Tara's pointy ears sticking out of her silken hair. "You don't look like the usual travel companions."

"Like I said, she's from a different place."

"How did you happen upon one another?"

"The portal was in a waterfall not far from my treehouse. I saw her while I was foraging for food."

"Have you gone back to this waterfall?"

"Yes, but the portal is no longer there."

"I see," the warlock nodded, turning his attention toward Clover.

"Was there anything distinctive about this waterfall?"

"No," Clover said. "It was just a normal waterfall, like you'd find anywhere in the forest."

The warlock squinted his eyes at Clover's tight sheepskin suit, running his eyes up and down her long, creamy legs.

"And were you wearing those clothes when you entered from the other side?"

"No, I wasn't wearing anything at all."

"Do you make a habit of traipsing through the forest completely naked?"

"I...just stopped to take a refreshing shower," Clover stammered, feeling increasingly uncomfortable with the warlock's line of questioning and his leering body language.

"Um-hmm," the warlock nodded with a slight curl forming on one side of his mouth. "Is there anything else you can tell me about the features of this waterfall or what you were doing before you fell through the portal?"

"Um..." Clover paused, peering at Tara unsteadily.

"I'll need every detail if you expect me to find this portal," the warlock said. "In my experience, there's always some special circumstances that makes it appear. Were you thinking or wishing about anything unusual while you were under the waterfall?"

Clover peered over at Tara again, noticing her hand resting defensively on her knife holster. Then she nodded, indicating that Clover should proceed.

"I–I was *touching* myself," she said. "The water was quite stimulating, and I couldn't help myself."

"I see," the warlock smiled. "And at what point did the portal appear?"

"After I climaxed," Clover said. "I fell backward, and instead of the hard wall, there was only an open field. A field in this new land of Abbynthia."

"Alright then," the warlock nodded. "This is very helpful."

"Can you help me?" Clover said. "Can you help me find the location of the magic portal, or create a new one for me to get back home?"

"I think so," the warlock said. "But I'll need some kind of token from your homeland to conjure the spell."

"What *kind* of token?" Clover said. "I left all my personal belongings at the base of the waterfall on the other side."

"Hmm," the warlock hummed, stroking his beard. "Then I'll need a lock of your hair. You apparently brought *that* much with you, didn't you?"

"Yes," Clover said, peering at the warlock suspiciously. "Do you have some scissors?"

"One moment," the man said, standing to retrieve some shears from his kitchen cabinet.

When he returned, he handed them to Clover and she tilted her head down to clip off a few strands.

"From *below*," the warlock said, glancing toward her crotch.

"*What*?" Clover said with wide eyes. "Why is that necessary?"

"We need to recreate the precise circumstances of your departure from the other world. And some kind of physical object that closely mirrors your desires at the moment of passing."

"I don't know about this," Clover said, peering over at Tara who was shaking her head in hesitation. "I don't feel comfortable removing my clothes in front of you."

"You can use the washroom down the hall if you're feeling shy. It doesn't matter how you provide the material, but I'll need it one way or the other if you wish to proceed."

Clover glanced toward Tara, shaking her head in doubt, then Tara nodded softly.

"We'll give this so-called *warlock* a tiny bit of room to maneuver," she said, rising from her chair and placing an arrow in her bow, pointing it toward the floor. "You go ahead. I'll make sure this guy doesn't get any other ideas."

"You're worrying unnecessarily," Aramiss said. "I can't produce the required spell without the necessary ingredients. It just so happens that in this case, the key ingredient is something a little more intimate."

Tara motioned toward the washroom in the rear of the house as she peered at the warlock with the same steely gaze she'd given the ratcatchers at the tavern. Feeling more secure in taking her leave, Clover excused herself and closed the door behind her in the washroom, delicately snipping off a lock near the top of her bush.

When she returned, the warlock placed the lock of hair in a large bowl on his kitchen table, then he added some spices and potions from the bottles on his shelves before pouring some boiling water into the bowl and stirring it gently. He closed his eyes and swiped his hands in the direction of his face, directing the steam toward his nostrils as he breathed in the scent.

Clover grimaced as she peered over at Tara, shaking her head at the magician's strange methods. But as he continued to wave his hands over the steaming bowl, suddenly the girls began to feel faint and within a matter of seconds, they fell limp onto the floor.

When they woke up, they found themselves naked and tied spreadeagled to the posts of the warlock's upstairs bed with their hips facing one another. As they flailed helplessly against their bonds, the warlock sneered at them with a toothy grin.

"What are you *doing* to us?" Clover said, feeling the leather straps digging into her wrists.

"I'm completing the incantation, of course," the warlock

smiled. "We have to recreate the conditions as closely as they existed before you fell through the portal. The only thing missing is your climax. I figured you'd be more comfortable on the bed stimulating yourself."

"I'm not going to rub my pussy with you watching, you pervert!" Clover hissed, thrashing on the bed trying to loosen her bonds.

"Perhaps your *girlfriend* can help you then," he said, peering at the two girls' naked vulvas only inches apart. "I can tell you two like each other more than regular acquaintances. It can't be so bad, can it? All you have to do is pleasure yourself while I watch, so I can invoke the incantation at the right moment. You'll be back home in no time."

"I don't *believe* you!" Clover said, pushing her hips up and down, causing the bed to shake and groan.

"Yes, just like that," the warlock smiled. "Is that the way you shook your hips when you climaxed under the waterfall?"

"I'll have your *balls* for this," Tara said, sneering at the old man.

"You might have my balls in *another* way if you're not too careful," the warlock said. "You're in no position to make idle threats right now."

"We're not going to do anything to satisfy your perverted fantasies," Tara said. "And when we're out of here, the local sheriff will lock you up and throw away the key."

"You're presuming you're actually getting *out* of here," the warlock smiled. "After the pretty redhead returns home, perhaps I'll keep you chained to my bed as my personal slave."

"You'll *never* touch me, you sick bastard!" Tara said, twisting frantically on the bed.

"We'll see about that," the man said, approaching the cot as he began to unbuckle his pants.

"*Help, help!*" Clover screamed, realizing the two women were in an impossible situation from which they couldn't free themselves.

"I'm afraid screaming won't help," the warlock said, dropping his pants to the floor and pulling off his robes. "We're a long way from town and hundreds of feet from the road. Nobody can hear you out here in the woods."

"Eeeeee!" Clover suddenly shrieked at the top of her lungs, like she did when she was a little girl being chased by her brothers.

The warlock winced from the painful sound in his ears and he leaned forward, slapping Clover across the face.

"*Shut up!*" he sneered. "Or I'll fuck you in *all* your holes before I'm finished with you. We can do this the easy way or the hard way."

"Leave Clover alone," Tara said, thrashing wildly against her straps. "Take me if you must. If you're looking for a quick roll, I'll work just as well as her."

"How touching," the warlock said. "But it's the *redhead* who needs the special stimulation if she hopes to get home."

He poured some of the potion from the mixing bowl onto Clover's stomach and began rubbing it down over her hips and between her thighs.

"We just need to get her properly lubricated to get her in the mood. But don't worry, I'll come for you when I'm finished with her."

As he kneeled on the bed between the two pinned women, positioning himself between Clover's legs with his dripping organ inches away from her quivering body, he suddenly reared up with a grimace on his face, howling in pain. Clover looked up and noticed a young man standing behind him, holding a sword in his hand. As he lurched toward the warlock with the blade extended in front of him, Aramiss extended the palm of his hand in the young man's direction, sending a bolt of energy flinging him against the far wall.

"What do we have here?" the warlock sneered at the trembling youth. "The third musketeer? It's too bad your sword is no match for my magic powers. But you're welcome to stay and watch while I service your girlfriends. Or do you want to get in on the action too?"

As the warlock directed his palm toward the young man, a beam of light shot out from his hand while he slowly lifted it higher, raising the boy helplessly against the wall of the bedroom.

"Now stay there like a good little boy while I finish my business. Perhaps you'll learn a thing or two watching me. You barely look old enough to have lost your virginity. I'm probably doing you a favor showing you how to do it properly."

Fortunately, all the extra commotion on the bed had loosened Clover's bonds enough to free her left foot, and with all the strength she could muster, she directed her gaze toward the warlock's hairy balls dangling between his legs, administering a swift kick to his crotch. As he collapsed onto the floor doubled over in pain, his spell over the young man was temporarily broken and the boy fell back onto the floor, retrieving his sword. Within seconds he covered the distance between him and the warlock and raised his weapon in the air, slicing off Aramiss's head in one quick motion.

As the warlock's body crumpled to the floor with his vacant-eyed head rolling beside him, the two girls peered up at their savior with wide eyes. Whether it was from shock at the intruder's sudden appearance or from their relief at being saved from the warlock's lascivious intentions, neither was sure. They were just happy to have another man in the room, one who was decidedly better smelling and looking than the craggy-nosed warlock.

7

———

"Who are you?" Tara said as the young man began to untie the girls' constraints.

"My name's Jessop."

"What are you doing here? How did you happen upon this house and hear our cries for help?"

"I followed you here," Jessop said, turning his back as the girls put their clothes back on. "I saw what happened at the tavern and thought you might need some protection until you got out of town."

Tara peered at the intruder suspiciously, annoyed that he'd been watching them so closely. Especially a handsome *human* boy whom Clover couldn't seem to take her eyes off.

"We can look after ourselves just fine," she said.

"That's not the way it appeared to me," he said, motioning to the dead warlock with his pants around his ankles.

"What do we do now?" Clover said, sidestepping the pool of blood forming on the floor. "Shouldn't we inform the authorities? I mean, we just committed murder."

"It wasn't *murder*," Tara said. "It was self-defense. And the sooner we get out of here the better. We don't need any more unwanted attention in these parts. The warlock got what he deserved, and if we leave now, no one will be any the wiser. The only other person who knows what happened here is Jessop."

Clover peered at Jessop then back at Tara and sighed.

"You guys seem to live by a different moral code in this land. Where are you from, Jessop?"

"I was born in the Norseland but stowed away aboard a commercial sailing vessel. When it docked in a nearby port, I figured this was as good as any place to get off."

"You seem pretty handy with a sword," Clover said, appraising his sinewy figure under his tight-fitting clothes. "Especially for someone so young. Where did you learn those skills?"

"My father's a lord in the Kingdom of Stordalen. I've received fencing lessons since a young age."

"If your father is a *lord*, why did you feel the need to run away?" Tara said, still wary of the young man's intentions.

"I'm his only son. He expected me to take over the estate and look after the lands and vassals under his command. I grew tired of all the rules and responsibilities."

"You gave up all those riches and a cushy life for *this*?" Tara said, sweeping her hand around the warlock's modest abode.

"I guess I wanted to make my own way in the world," he said. "I don't like having someone else telling me what I can do or where I can go. I'm a bit of a free spirit."

"Welcome to the club," Clover chuckled. "It's funny how we three renegades bumped into each other."

"It's not so funny when someone gets *killed*," Tara said, glancing at the lifeless body of the warlock.

"So what do we do now?" Clover said.

"We get as far away from here as possible," Tara said. "As quickly as possible."

"What about *Jessop*?" Clover said.

"What *about* him?"

"He saved our lives!"

"He may have saved us from *something*," Tara nodded. "But he may have also ruined your best chance at getting back home."

"Do you really think that warlock was legit? Maybe this whole scheme was just a ruse to get into our pants."

"I guess we'll never know now, will we?"

"What about *you*, Jessop?" Clover said, peering back at the handsome drifter. "What are your plans now?"

"I don't really have any," he said. "I figured I'd just follow my nose and see what new adventures I might find along the way."

"Adventures seem to follow us everywhere we go. Why don't you tag along with us for a little while? It wouldn't hurt to have a man with your skills join us if you don't have anywhere else to go."

Clover glanced at Tara with puppy dog eyes.

"What do you think, Tara?"

Tara looked at the young swordsman then back at Clover, pausing.

"Maybe just for a little while. At least until we get far enough away from here to know it's safe. But don't get any frisky ideas, Romeo. The last thing we need is another randy joker trying to make a pass at us. I think we've had plenty enough of those kinds of distractions for a while."

"I wouldn't *think* of it," Jessop said, trying to keep his eyes from wandering down to soak up the two girls' sexy figures.

The three friends headed north for a few hours, then built a campfire and bedded down for the night. There was a slight chill in the air, and as the two girls nestled up against one another to keep warm, Clover peered over at Jessop, wondering how much longer he'd stay with their little troupe. Although she'd grown quite fond of Tara, she still hadn't experienced the pleasures of being with a man, and as she reflected back on her exciting experience in the erotic forest, she felt a new stirring in her loins.

In the morning, the three explorers enjoyed a hearty breakfast of rabbit and quail eggs, then they packed up their gear and hesitated, trying to figure out where to go next.

"So where do we go now?" Clover said, frowning. "We're still no closer to finding my magic portal, and I have no idea how to get back home."

"You said the portal was in a *waterfall*, right?" Jessop said, recalling the details of their adventure that the girls had shared with him over breakfast. "Waterfalls are generally located in the mountains, so it stands to reason that we should head up to higher terrain. Maybe you just need to find the *right* waterfall."

"That's as good a plan as any," Tara said. "It's not like my treehouse was a permanent residence, anyway. I was just hanging out there until I found a better reason to leave."

Clover smiled as the trio began winding their way through the forest, following a narrow river upstream toward the highlands. She was thrilled that Tara was happy to stay with her until she found her way back home, and having Jessop join them made the journey all the more exciting. She'd always enjoyed exploring the forest with her brothers, and now she had a new travel companion that made her feel some unfamiliar new sensations.

After a few hours, the group paused at the opening to a clearing when they heard an unusual sound. It was a deep and husky noise, like it came from a bear or some other large animal. But the panting and growling sounded *labored*, like the animal was in distress. As they inched closer to the noise, they crouched down, noticing a large animal heaving next to a fallen log.

"What *is* that?" Clover said, staring at the hulking form.

"Is that what I think it is?" Jessop said, peering more closely.

"Oh my God," Tara said. "I think it's a dragon!"

"A dragon!?" Clover squealed. "I can't believe we actually found one!"

"Shh!" Tara said, placing her finger on Clover's lips. "We don't want to attract its attention. Dragons and humans aren't exactly best friends."

"Or *elves*, for that matter," Jessop said. "We might make a tasty snack for him if he catches us. Let's double back and take a wide berth around this thing. There's no need sticking our noses in someone else's business where it doesn't belong."

As Tara and Jessop stood to head in the opposite direction, Clover suddenly reached out, grabbing Tara's vest.

"Wait!" she said. "It looks like it's hurt. Maybe we can help it."

"*Help* it?" Tara said. "There's a novel idea. Humans wanting to *help* a dragon instead of slaying it. Are you crazy?"

"We can at least get a little closer to see what's wrong with it," Clover said. "Maybe it's pinned under the log and we can help free it."

"And then what? Watch it fly away as it flaps its wings at

us in gratitude? Or stand helplessly by while it burns us to a crisp with its dragon breath?"

"It won't hurt to *look* at least. As long as we're careful approaching the creature so it doesn't see or hear us."

Tara looked at Jessop with a bewildered look on her face, trying to divine his thoughts. He peered back at her and shrugged his shoulders.

"Let's approach it from upwind," he nodded. "At least that way he won't smell us coming."

The trio circled around the clearing and as they began approaching the dragon from the other direction, Clover suddenly gasped, holding up her hand to stop their progress.

"Look!" she said. "It's got a spear embedded in one of its wings! No wonder he's whining and panting. Can't we do anything for him?"

"You mean like walk up to him and yank it out?" Tara said, looking at Clover like she had two heads. "He'll probably mistake us for another dragon slayer and fry us to a crisp before we get within a hundred feet of him."

"Maybe we can wait until he's *asleep* or something," Clover said. "There's got to be *some* way we can help him."

Tara paused for a moment to contemplate their predicament. Then she reached into her pouch and pulled out a handful of dried leaves.

"There might be one thing we can do. Before we left the warlock's house, I took a handful of those potions he used to drug us. Maybe if we use *enough* of them, we can induce the dragon to fall asleep long enough for us to safely remove the spear."

"That's a great idea!" Clover said, jumping up and down excitedly.

"It's not without its risks though," Tara said, peering over at Jessop. "There's no telling if the creature might wake up while we're trying to pull out the arrow and gobble us alive. Are you up for this, Jessop? We might need a distraction if the dragon wakes up too soon."

Jessop peered at the two girls with wide eyes, then nodded slowly.

"Sure," he said. "I said I was looking for new adventures. This sounds about as crazy an escapade as any."

"Okay," Tara said. "Let's build a fire a few hundred feet upstream, then we can boil some water and add the potions to create an intoxicating vapor. Hopefully when the dragon inhales it, it'll be enough to put him to sleep."

"What will we use to boil the water?" Clover said. "We don't have any kind of pot to place over the fire."

"Don't worry about that right now," Tara said. "I've done this sort of thing before. Let's get upriver where it will be safer to build a fire."

Tara led them to an area with some large gray rocks by the riverbank, then she kneeled down and picked one up that was about a foot in diameter.

"This is soft shale," she said. "I'll get started chipping it into a makeshift bowl if you guys can get started making a fire."

"I don't know how to make a fire," Clover said, shaking her head. "I usually use matches or a lighter back home."

"A *what*?" Tara said, looking at her with a wrinkled forehead.

"Right, sorry," Clover said, shaking her head. "I forgot you guys are stuck in the stone ages."

"What about you, Jessop?" Tara said, peering at their new friend. "Did your father teach you any *other* useful survival skills?"

"No problem," he said. "It might take me a while, but I should be able to scare one up in twenty minutes or so."

While Jessop went to find some dry sticks and a dowel to make a fire, Clover knelt down beside Tara watching her chip away at the soft shale rock with a harder granite stone. The rock began to splinter into shears, and as she swept away the broken pieces, the large round rock slowly began to form a hollow in the middle. Within a half hour or so, she'd created large bowl shape in the stone.

She peered over at Jessop rubbing his hands together over a stick resting on a dry piece of wood, and after a short while, some tendrils of smoke began rising off the surface. Jessop threw some dry moss over the smoke then knelt down to blow on it and it erupted into a small flame. He threw some larger sticks onto the pile, then nodded toward Tara who was grinding the finishing touches on her stone bowl.

"Jesus," Clover sighed, kneeling down in front of them as they constructed a firepit from some larger logs to boil the water. "You really know what you're doing out here in the wilderness. I feel like such a lightweight around you guys."

"You're useful for one or two things when the need arises," Tara said, smiling at Clover. "Who else would have dreamed up the idea of saving an injured dragon?"

Tara placed some river water in the bowl, then poured in the bag of spices she'd taken from the warlock's house and stirred it gently in the stone pot until it came to a bowl.

"Let's hope this'll do the trick," she said, blowing the steam away from their noses. "When we get close enough to the dragon, one of you will need to use some kind of flap to fan the steam in the dragon's direction."

"Flap?" Clover said.

"Like a piece of clothing. You've got the largest piece with your one-piece bodysuit. Jessop will just have to look in the other direction while you flap your sheepskin in the buff."

The two girls glanced up at Jessop with a raised eyebrow, and he peered back at them like a kid who'd just been caught fishing around his sister's underwear drawer.

"Sure," he smiled, glancing at Clover's spilling bosom. "Whatever it takes to help the cause."

The trio tiptoed to within a safe distance of the panting dragon then knelt down in the long grass. The dragon had its eyes closed, groaning in obvious pain.

"We going to have to do this fast, before the steam disappears," Tara said. "It's now or never."

Clover removed her bodysuit while Jessop turned his head in the other direction, then the two girls raised themselves as high above the grass as they dared while Clover flapped the steam from the pot in the dragon's direction. The vapor wafted downwind, and the dragon slowly began to breathe more softly until his body fell limp.

"Do you think the potion was strong enough to put him to sleep?" Clover said, peering at dragon more carefully.

"I guess we're about to find out," she said, pulling her knife out of her holster. "I'm going to need you two to provide a distraction if he wakes up while I'm trying to remove the spear. Let's keep our fingers crossed that this works."

"And every *other* body part," Clover said, trying to protect her modesty standing in the tall grass totally naked.

As Tara crept closer to the dragon, Clover and Jessop watched her with wide eyes, holding their breath hoping the creature wouldn't awaken. Clover didn't even bother to put her clothes back on as she held Jessop's hand tightly, feeling the sheath of his rigid sword pressing against her bare hips.

When Tara got within arm's length of the dragon, she reached out to delicately touch the side of its flanks, and it didn't stir. Nodding back in the direction of her friends, she began to climb over its injured wing, squatting in front of the thick spear embedded in its wing. Fortunately, the point hadn't sunk too deep into its flesh, just far enough to keep the barb embedded under its thick scaly skin, making it impossible to fly.

As she slowly sliced around the wound with her hunting knife, being careful not to deepen the gash any further, she stood up and tried to pull the lance out of the dragon's wing. When it finally popped out, the dragon flinched, and Tara froze in fear, glancing toward its head. When she noticed it was still sleeping, she drew a needle and thread she kept in her pouch for emergency first aid and did her best to stich up the foot-wide gash. But just as she hopped off the dragon with the spear in her hand, it stirred and opened its eyes. When he saw Tara standing next to him carrying the spear, he reared up and opened his mouth preparing to spray Tara with its fire.

Suddenly, Clover and Jessop began jumping up and down in the field a few feet away, and the dragon peered at them like a curious dog, tilting its head in confusion. When he peered back at Tara, she threw the spear onto the ground to show that she wasn't a threat, and her companions emerged from the grass, holding their arms over their heads in mock surrender. The dragon peered at Clover's naked body and her flowing red locks, tilting its head to the other side.

Tara crept up to the dragon's face and patted it softly, and the creature peered back at its injured wing and flapped it gently, noticing the spear was no longer causing it pain. He peered back at the trio and purred softly, seeming to realize that they'd been responsible for removing the weapon while he was sleeping.

"Look!" Clover said, approaching the dragon slowly while Jessop followed gingerly behind. "He *likes* us! I think it worked. Were you able to close the wound?"

"I did the best I could," Tara nodded. "If he heals anything like the rest of us, he should be ready to fly in another couple of days."

"What do we do in the meantime?" Clover said, moving closer to the dragon as it swiped its nose gently against her naked body.

"Well for one thing," she said, noticing Jessop staring at Clover's naked ass. "You should probably get dressed before this dragon gets any other ideas. If we've learned anything in the last couple of days, it's that we can't trust anything with a cock when we get too close."

8

———

For the next few days, the trio stayed with the dragon, tending to its wound and feeding it wild boar and as much fruit and vegetables as they could find on the hillsides. It seemed to be improving each day, flapping its wings more vigorously and eagerly awaiting their foraging trips from the field. After Clover said he looked like a dinosaur with wings, they decided to name him Rex.

One afternoon, as the team was out collecting provisions in a meadow, Clover noticed Jessop straying from the group and hiding behind a tree. Curious as to what he was doing, she crept up behind him and her eyes widened when she saw his naked ass thrusting into a knot in the tree. Not long after, Tara pulled up beside her, and the two girls smiled at one another.

"Poor thing," Tara whispered. "He's got no other outlet for his adolescent urges."

"It looks like Medusa offers a pretty tempting target for him," Clover said, listening to Jessop moaning as he plowed his shiny cock in and out of the slippery hole.

"The tree giveth and the tree taketh," Tara chuckled.

As Jessop grew increasingly animated thrusting his hips against the tree, the overhanging branches dangled against his ass, curling underneath to tickle his testicles with their feathery leaves. He wrapped his arms around the smooth skin of the trunk and made one final deep thrust, groaning loudly. When he pulled his pulsing organ out of the tree and the girls saw how well-endowed he was, they gasped. Jessop turned his head in their direction and they ducked under the tall grass, giggling.

"Maybe we can help him with that a little later," Clover said. "We've both enjoyed the pleasures of the erotic mushroom, and that looks like a much more tempting skewer to bounce up and down on."

"He's certainly been staring at our *asses* plenty enough since we joined up with him," Tara nodded. "And he *is* kind of cute. Maybe we can let him snuggle up beside us tonight for a little extra warmth while we give him a little *two-way* attention?"

As Jessop tracked back through the field in their direction, they lowered themselves in the grass then followed him back to their camp.

"Did you find any special treats for our dragon friend to enjoy on your foraging trip?" Tara teased, glancing at Jessop with a sly grin.

"Um, yes," Jessop stammered, spilling a bag of fruits and vegetables in front of Rex's face as he eagerly gobbled them up. "I'm just not sure it'll be enough to satisfy his voracious appetite."

"No doubt," Tara snickered.

She climbed up on Rex's back to inspect his wound and spread some soothing aloe oil over it as the dragon purred.

"The wound is almost healed," she said, hopping back

down onto the ground. "He should be ready to fly again by tomorrow with any luck."

"It's too bad, really," Clover said, rubbing her face against his soft nose. "I've grown kind of attached to him these past few days. And the feeling seems to be mutual."

"Well, we can't exactly keep him as a *pet*," Tara said, stroking his scaly skin. "These creatures were meant to soar. We'd just be holding him back from his natural tendencies if we keep spoon-feeding him like this."

"I suppose you're right," Clover said, giggling as Rex licked the front of her body with his long tongue.

"Let's see if the two of us can scare up another boar for supper while Jessop prepares the fire," Tara said. "It'll be good for Rex to have a full belly before he heads back out on his own."

As the two women headed out into the bush, Clover raised the new bow Tara had made for her, snaring a snorting boar as it stampeded through the brush. She'd also become more adept at using her new whip, stunning small game and rodents from a distance of twenty feet with a quick crack of her lash. When they carried the boar and three rabbits back to the camp on a large pole, Rex wagged his tail excitedly, licking his lips as he drooled onto the ground.

The four of them enjoyed the roast game around the campfire, then they nestled up together like they usually did to turn in for the night. When the girls saw Jessop take up his customary position on the opposite side of Rex and curl up to go to sleep, Tara elbowed Clover in the side and nodded at her with a knowing smile.

"Why don't you come over and join us on *this* side tonight, Jessop?" she called. "It's closer to the fire and we could use the extra warmth."

"Okay," Jessop said, hardly losing a moment to switch positions.

When he lay down beside the girls, Tara rolled over, pinning him between the two of them.

"We saw what you were doing in the forest today," she said, caressing the side of his leg.

"While I was foraging for food, you mean?" he said.

"Yes," she purred. "But it wasn't just *food* you were looking for, was it?"

"You were spying on me?"

"It wasn't hard to miss, with you moaning and pounding the tree like that."

"I just got a little–"

"No need to explain," Tara said, drawing her hand up around his hardening pole and squeezing his balls. "We know the feeling. You're not the *only* one who likes to play with the erotic plants."

"I was beginning to wonder," he said. "You're both so beautiful and it seems such a shame for all of that to go to waste..."

"Oh?" Tara smiled. "Do you think you can help us satisfy our feminine needs? Have you ever been with a woman before?"

"Well, I–"

"He *hasn't!*" Clover smiled, caressing the inside of his opposite thigh. "What about two women at the *same time*?"

"Oh my God," Jessop groaned as he felt Tara begin to unbuckle his belt.

"That's right, sweetie," she said, blowing into his ear. "Tonight, we're going to show what it feels like to put your pecker into something a little warmer and wetter than a tree."

As Tara pulled his pants down to his ankles, Clover

stared at his big prick gleaming in the moonlight, pulsing excitedly in synchronicity with his thumping pulse.

"That's quite an impressive instrument you've got there," Tara said, wrapping her fist around his manhood while she smiled at Clover. "I think you've got enough to satisfy *both* of us with that thing. How do you want to do this, Clover? Do you want first dibs, or me?"

"Maybe we can have some fun playing with him at the *same time*, like we did with the two-headed mushroom in the forest."

"But he's only got one penis."

"Yes, but we have two pussies."

Tara peered at Clover with a puzzled expression, then she nodded, catching her drift. While Clover rolled on top of Jessop, rubbing her tits against his furry chest, Tara turned herself around and lay on her back with her pussy pressed up against his balls. When he felt the two women's vulvas sandwiching his twitching dick and begin rocking their hips together, he groaned as Clover pressed her lips against his, rolling her tongue in his mouth.

"Are you enjoying this, Jess?" Tara said. "Is it better than fucking an inanimate tree?"

"*Fuck* yes," Jessop panted.

"Show him what a real woman's pussy feels like, Clover," Tara said, feeling his lubrication dribbling down over his balls. "I think he needs to sheath that sword before he spills his seed again where it doesn't belong."

Clover raised her hips over Jessop's erection and tilted her hips, pointing it into her dripping hole. When she lowered her pussy over his entire length, they groaned into each other's mouths. As Clover began to rock her hips up and down over his burning pole, Tara felt her slippery ass rubbing against her own sex, and she grasped Jessop's thighs, pulling herself harder against his balls.

Jessop groaned from the pleasure of two wet pussies stimulating every part of his lower region, and as Clover's juices began to pour down over Tara's slit, she began to finger her hard nub watching Jessop's cock pounding in an out of Clover's hole. As the three of them began to shake their bodies together and moan more loudly, the dragon started to stir, twitching his wing over their flapping bodies.

"We better get this over with before Rex gets some ideas of his own," Tara said. "I don't think we're going to be able to satisfy his much larger organ if he gets any more distracted."

"No worries," Clover panted, flapping her hips harder against Jessop's cock. "I'm almost there. *Come* with me, Jessop. Your cock feels so good inside my pussy."

Jessop wrapped his arms around Clover's back and pulled her harder toward him, then he titled his hips, burying his balls deep into her quivering hole. As they began moaning in simultaneous climax, Tara pressed her pussy hard up against Jessop's balls, squirting her juices against his anus and Clover's quivering buttocks. While they wailed in simultaneous union, Rex suddenly rolled over to his side and they felt an enormous throbbing projection poking them from behind.

———

I n the morning, the three friends got up and fried bacon and quail eggs in their makeshift frypan while they peered over at Rex who was licking their plateful of scraps pensively.

"I think he's ready to go," Tara said, noticing him flapping his wings restlessly. "If last night was anything to go by, he needs to find some more of his *own* kind to satisfy his wanderlust. We certainly can't attend to *all* of his needs."

"I agree," Clover said, peering at his enormous dragon genitals dangling between his hind legs. "But how do we encourage him to go? I think we might have trained him a little too well to rely on us to give him regular food."

"Maybe if we push or prod him, he'll get the message," Tara said, walking over to the dragon and trying to push him to get up off his haunches.

While Jessop did the same thing on the other side, Clover flapped her arms in front of him, trying to encourage him to take flight. After a few moments, he stood up on his hind legs and began to flap his wings as the trio nodded their heads excitedly, raising their hands in the air signaling for him to take flight.

He began to flap his wings faster and faster, and after a few moments he rose his weight off the ground, lifting himself a few feet above his friends. They ducked down from the force of the heavy draft produced by his enormous wings, and as he lifted himself higher up, he flew off a short distance, soaring and angling his body to test his wings, seeming to enjoy putting on a show for his friends while they hooted and clapped excitedly from the ground.

But instead of flying off into the distance, after a few minutes of demonstrating his acrobatic skills, he flew back towards them and landed a few feet away, sitting on his hind legs like a happy puppy.

"It looks like he doesn't want to leave," Tara said, shaking her head at the panting dragon.

"What do we do now?" Jessop said. "We can't exactly put him on a leash, and he'll lose us in the forest when he's flying so far overhead."

"Maybe we can catch a *ride* with him," Clover said. "We'll

have an eagle eye's view of the terrain from up there and he can help us find the location of all the waterfalls in the region. We can certainly cover a lot more ground from up above than hacking our way through the forest."

"You're *full* of nutty ideas, aren't you?" Tara said, shaking her head. "How will we steer him? I've never exactly ridden a dragon before."

"People probably thought the same thing when they first got on a horse," Clover said. "We'll just play it by ear. Hopefully he'll learn our cues over time and we'll figure out how to send him the right signals."

"What will we hold onto?" Jessop asked. "We can't exactly put a saddle on this thing."

"He's got plenty of large scales. We can wedge our feet under the plates and use them like a stirrup while we hold onto the bony spikes of his neck like the horn of a saddle."

"You make it sound like it's going to be as easy as riding a horse!" Tara said.

"We'll never know until we give it a try. We said we were looking for adventures. I bet nobody's tried anything like *this* before."

The three friends paused as they peered at one another, then they slowly climbed up onto Rex's back as he lowered himself onto the ground like a kneeling camel. Clover got on first, with Tara immediately behind her, and Jessop taking up the rear. She positioned herself behind the last bony spike on his neck, then curled her toes underneath two large scales on his flanks while her friends mimicked her technique. Then Clover slapped her heels gently against Rex's flanks, and he flapped his wings, gingerly lifting the three of them off the ground.

As he took flight, their eyes widened watching the terrain disappear below them, and before long Rex was swooping through the air, gleefully giving his friends the ride of their life while they whooped and hollered on his back. Clover experimented by gently pulling on his ears and shifting her weight forward and back to steer him like an airplane, and before long he adapted to her signals, turning, soaring, and diving like a giant eagle.

After an hour or so, the band noticed a flock of large birds approaching them from the West, and they peered at the strange creatures as Rex began to huff uncomfortably.

"What are *those* things?" Jessop said, squinting into the sun.

"Gargoyles," Tara said, pinching Clover's side.

"*Gargoyles*?" Clover said. "Holy hell, what are we going to run into next? What do they want with us?"

"I don't know," Tara said, but I don't think we should stick around to find out. "There's a lot more of them than us."

Clover pulled on Rex's left ear to signal him to turn East, but when he saw the threatening band of beasts massing toward them, he tilted his body, flying directly in their direction.

"Where are you going?!" Tara screamed into Clover's ear, suddenly worried for her safety.

"It's not my idea," she said. "Rex seems to have a mind of his own."

As they got closer to the strange beasts, Clover noticed they had muscular physiques like a lion, but with the articulated wings and ugly faces of giant bats. As Rex flew straight toward the pack, he reared his head back, bellowing a long stream of fire directly at them, causing them to splice off and circle around. As they got closer, Rex used his longer wings to bat them out of the sky one by one, and after frying a few more of the brutes into a crisp, they bugged out in the other direction.

Having had enough excitement for the day, Clover peered down looking for a safe place to land, noticing a large castle in the distance. As they circled high overhead, she peered back at Tara.

"Do you know what that place is?" she said.

"I don't know for sure, but it looks huge, even from this height. I think it might be the Kingdom of Gargaton. I've heard rumors about a place where everybody is ten times the size of normal people. The king would hold a lot of power in this land and know many things about the region. Perhaps he can give you some more clues about the location of your magic waterfall."

"What do you say, Jessop? Clover said, peering back at their new sidekick. "Are you game for taking a closer look?"

"Sure," he said. "We've got a *dragon* to protect us, right? What could possibly go wrong?"

Clover pulled gently on the right side of Rex's neck and leaned her body forward, signaling for him to move closer to the castle. But the closer they got, the more enormous it appeared, with Rex beginning to look more like a large *horsefly* buzzing around the soaring ramparts than a scary dragon.

"Let's go down on the ground to check this out more closely," Clover said, steering Rex toward the large front gate surrounded by a wide moat.

When they landed outside the imposing facade, they peered up at the enormous wooden doors rising almost a hundred feet overhead. They knelt down to peer under the base of the gates, then opened their eyes in shock as a horse with hooves as big as tractor tires clomped noisily past. There was a buzz of activity in the courtyard as giant people carried provisions across the dusty piazza while children bigger than their dragon scurried around kicking a ball.

"Wow," Clover said, pulling back and peering at her friends with wide eyes. "You weren't kidding about these people. They're *huge*! How do you think they'll react to the intrusion of little people like us?"

"We can't be seen as much of *threat* to them, that's for sure," Tara said. "They're either going to view us a curiosity or as a tasty snack for their afternoon tea. We should definitely proceed with caution if we're going to try to make contact."

"How should we go about doing this?" Clover said, peering up at the castle walls. "Should we go in through the front gate or have Rex fly us up to one of those towers?"

"I don't know about you guys," Jessop said, noticing one of the giant horses dropping a steaming pile of manure onto the ground. "But I don't really feel like getting stepped on by one of those things. Besides, it's not just their *feet* we have to watch out for."

"It looks like Rex is going to prove himself useful in more ways than we thought," Clover said, smiling to her friends.

When she ran away from home only a few short days ago, she had no idea what new wonders and adventures awaited her in this strange new land of Abbynthia.

R eady for more erotic chills and thrills? Order the next exciting volume in Clover's Fantasy Adventures:

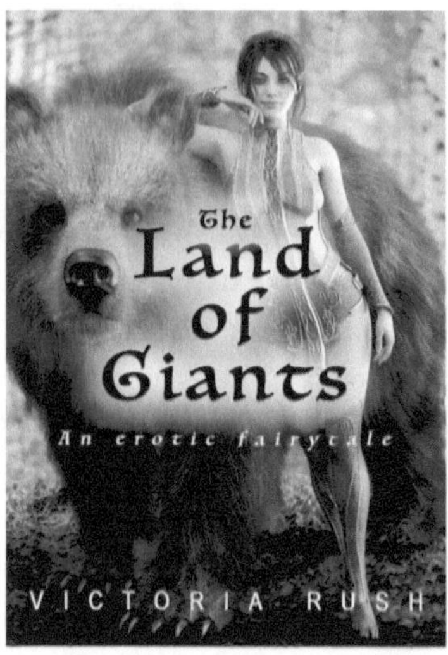

Being small sometimes has its advantages...

FOLLOW VICTORIA RUSH:

Want to keep informed of my latest erotic book releases? Sign up for my newsletter and receive a FREE bonus book:

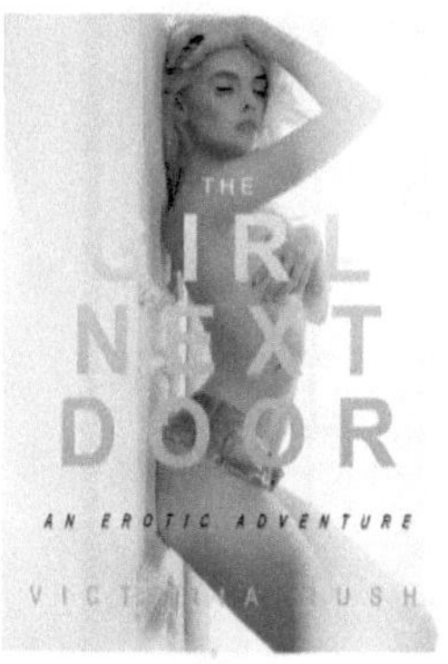

Spying on the neighbors just got a lot more interesting...